As you may remember, I've traveled pret[ty far from] home. Not because I wanted to, mind you[, but because] my Inchy self caught on some hiker's shoelace! It was pretty scary to be separated from Mom and Dad and places I was familiar with, but thank goodness I was invited to travel with Mrs. Ladybug. Things have been much better since we met. We love to talk as we travel, and that makes things quite interesting. She usually calls me, Inchy Dear, and lets me call her by her first and middle names…Lilly Louise. I'm learning a lot from Lilly Louise, and she says she's actually learning a lot from me. She says that's what happens when you have a good friend.

I must say that I still miss Mom and Dad. Even though I don't think of them quite as often as I used to, I still remember things they taught me, and try to always behave as a decent inchworm should...that's to be kind and helpful to other creatures, while at the same time being alert and careful in all my actions. It's a big job for a little creature, but it's the inch worm way. I remember Dad always saying, "Tiny creatures have HUMONGOUS responsibilities...and don't EVER forget that, Inchy." So, I think that's why I'm always looking around to see just what the heck is MY responsibility.

Just the other day, Lilly Louise and I were headed into the woods. She was remarking how beautiful the golden leaves were looking in the autumn sunlight. She usually notices things like that more than I do. Maybe that's because she sometimes flies a bit, and gets a better view of things. It takes me quite a while to inch up a tree, you know. Anyway, Lilly Lou had just commented on the golden leaves when I noticed something peculiar up ahead...

I rubbed my eyes, thinking I was imagining things, but, no, sure enough, it was something I did NOT expect to see.

"Lilly Louise," I called, "Would you come and look at this? I think it's a creature, but it seems to be wrapped tight in something."

I had never seen anything like it.

"Oh, my dear," she said, "Oh, I'm never happy to come upon something like this!"

"Something like what?" I asked. "What's happened?"

She explained how sometimes a grasshopper, who's usually very alert and quick, gets caught off guard, trapped by a spider and then wrapped tightly in its silk, only to later be served up as a tasty meal.

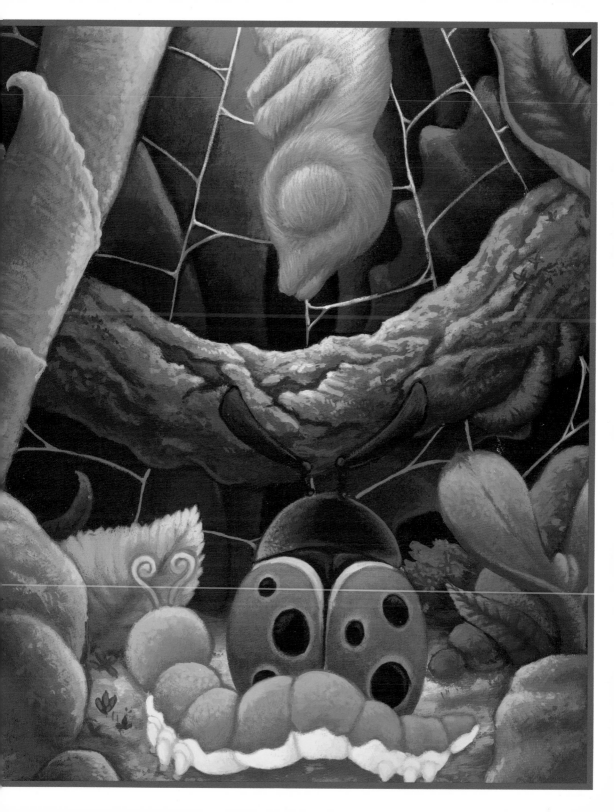

I thought for a moment, remembering how impolite and downright rude that old grasshopper had been to me when I was looking for a friend. But, hey, that was just him. It doesn't mean ALL grasshoppers are like that. What if this is a really friendly grasshopper? What if it's a mama grasshopper with little babies waiting at home for her return?

"AAAAHHHH!" I screamed. "We've got to help that grasshopper get free! Where's the spider?"

Lilly Louise flew up ahead to get a closer look. I kept on inching toward the trapped grasshopper, as fast as I could.

The closer I got, the more I thought. What could I do to help? I don't have strong cricket legs. I don't have sharp teeth like my big caterpillar cousins. I'm actually pretty tiny, you know...I probably won't be able to do a thing to help...I'm just a tiny little inch worm...I...I... I was stopped right in my tracks! What was it my Dad always told me? "Tiny creatures have HUMONGOUS responsibilities."

"Okay. That's right," I told myself, "I'm tiny, that's true. But, I'm HERE. And just like I was able to help Mrs. Ladybug, there MUST be a way I can help this grasshopper."

I had found another one of MY responsibilities.

From that point on, I was so very thoughtful of things that just might work to free that grasshopper. Lilly Louise flew back to meet me. She told me the creature was still alive, and the spider was sleeping a safe distance away. We discussed rescue possibilities all the way to the wrapped grasshopper.

The final plan was for Lilly Louise to fly in circles around the area, kind of as a lookout for the spider's awakening. My job was to chew and inch, chew and inch, back and forth along the same spot on the tight web surrounding the grasshopper. We figured that if I kept going back and forth over the same place, I'd eventually be able to cut through the thick silk just enough so the grasshopper could get free.

The grasshopper couldn't speak to us because the thick silky trap was covering its mouth, but we were hoping it could hear us, and we explained every move we were about to make.

"Good luck, my dear little Inchy," said Mrs. Ladybug as she flew up to begin her part of the rescue.

I inched up to the trapped grasshopper and began to inch and chew. The silky threads were tightly wound, and very sticky. My mouth got jammed up with web really often. Thank goodness I'm such a good spitter. I could ALWAYS spit further than any of the other inchworm kids. Mom never liked it when I'd spit, so I didn't do it TOO often, but, boy, for this rescue, it REALLY came in handy!

This inching, chewing, and spitting routine went on and on for hours, it seemed. My jaws were getting EXTREMELY tired. I stopped for just a minute or so to give myself a break, but every time I got a glance at that sleeping spider, I pushed myself to keep chewing. After all, we were trying to save a life!

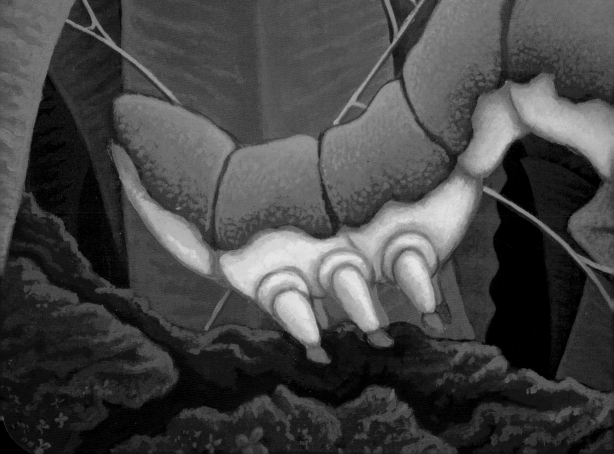

FINALLY! I could see one of the grasshopper's eyes looking down at me from under what was now a thin layer of web. Its mouth was almost free as well, and it actually was starting to make some sounds I could understand.

"Jolly good job," I understood it to say, "Keep going. Just a bit more."

I thought the voice sounded kind of familiar, but I wasn't quite sure. I looked more closely at the eye staring down at me, and...OH YES! It was. I was SURE it was. That same mean, impolite, downright RUDE, unfriendly old green leaf eating grasshopper who WOULDN'T be caught dead with ME...a little tiny inchworm who'd look "ridiculous" traveling with such an elegant grasshopper! Why that...

"Hey!" I shouted.

Just then the grasshopper burst the trap open, throwing me off the web and landing me flat on my back!

"Oooffff!" I heaved, as I landed onto a fallen leaf. It took me a minute to catch my breath.

As I looked up I saw the grasshopper, shaking himself and stretching. He noticed me on the ground, and leaned over to look me straight in the eye.

"Mr. Inch Worm it is, correct?" he asked. "I am forever in your debt, young worm. You have saved my precious life."

"Well," I said, a bit surprised at such a thank you, "I couldn't have done it without Mrs. Ladybug there, flying and keeping watch."

Lilly Louise saw the grasshopper was free and flew down to be with us.

"I do believe we've met before, Mr. Worm, have we not?" the grasshopper asked. "I was on my way to something rather important, was I not?"

"Yes, so you said. Something more important than making a friend anyway."

"Hhmm," he replied, "It appears as though I made quite a mistake. Do you think you could find it in your heart to forgive me?"

Of course you probably know that forgiving is something Mom and Dad taught me to always work at. They said it was the best thing to do if anyone ever did something that hurt me. Of course, they taught me to stand up for myself, but they said if I didn't forgive something bad, it would never ever go away...it would always be in my mind and keep hurting me every single day until I let it go by forgiving it. It sure is a big job sometimes, but I guess it is another one of MY responsibilities.

"I do forgive you, Mr. Grasshopper. We all make mistakes now and then, don't we?"

"Yes, we do, young worm. I must say, you and Mrs. Ladybug make an excellent rescue team. I thank you both for saving me. If there is ever an occasion where I may be of assistance to either of you...please do not hesitate to call out my name. I have quite excellent hearing, and I'll be with you as soon as I possibly can. And, please, you may call me Griswald, if you'd like."

GRISWALD! Jeesh! Why didn't that surprise me?

"Well, thank YOU, Mr. Gra..., ah, Griswald. I'm glad we were able to save your life."

"We'll remember your kind offer, Sir," said Lilly Louise.

"Please do," he replied, "Ta! Ta!"

And off he jumped. Probably going to some important affair he was now quite late for.